COOL Fish Recipes

Main Dishes for Beginning Chefs

Alex Kuskowski

South Huntington Public Library
145 Pidgeon Hill Road
Huntington Station, NY 11746

Checkerboard Library

An Imprint of Abdo Publishing
abdopublishing.com

abdopublishing.com

Published by Abdo Publishing, a division of ABDO, PO Box 398166, Minneapolis, Minnesota 55439. Copyright © 2017 by Abdo Consulting Group, Inc. International copyrights reserved in all countries. No part of this book may be reproduced in any form without written permission from the publisher. Checkerboard Library™ is a trademark and logo of Abdo Publishing.

Printed in the United States of America,
North Mankato, Minnesota
102016
012017

THIS BOOK CONTAINS RECYCLED MATERIALS

Design and Production: Mighty Media, Inc.
Series Editor: Liz Salzmann
Photo Credits: Mighty Media, Inc.; Shutterstock

The following manufacturers/names appearing in this book are trademarks: Kitchen Basics®, Oster®, Pyrex®, Roundy's®

Publisher's Cataloging-in-Publication Data

Names: Kuskowski, Alex, author.
Title: Cool fish recipes: main dishes for beginning chefs / by Alex Kuskowski.
Other titles: Main dishes for beginning chefs
Description: Minneapolis, MN : Abdo Publishing, 2017. | Series: Cool main dish recipes | Includes bibliographical references and index.
Identifiers: LCCN 2016944823 | ISBN 9781680781342 (lib. bdg.) | ISBN 9781680775549 (ebook)
Subjects: LCSH: Cooking--Juvenile literature. | Dinners and dining--Juvenile literature. | Entrees (Cooking)--Juvenile literature. | One-dish meals--Juvenile literature.
Classification: DDC 641.82--dc23
LC record available at http://lccn.loc.gov/2016944823

TO ADULT HELPERS

Get cooking! This is your chance to help a budding chef. Being able to cook meals is a life skill. Learning to cook gives kids new experiences and helps them gain confidence. These recipes are designed to help kids learn how to cook on their own. They may need more assistance on some recipes than others. Be there to offer guidance when they need it. Encourage them to do as much as they can on their own. Make sure to have rules for cleanup. There should always be adult supervision when kids are using sharp utensils or a hot oven or stove.

SAFETY FIRST!

Some recipes call for activities or ingredients that require caution. If you see these symbols, ask an adult for help.

HOT STUFF!
This recipe requires the use of a stove or oven. Always use pot holders when handling hot objects.

SUPER SHARP!
This recipe includes the use of a sharp utensil, such as a knife or grater.

NUT ALERT!
Some people can get very sick if they eat nuts. If you cook something with nuts, let people know!

Contents

Get the Dish on Fish!	4
I ♥ Fish	6
Cooking Basics	8
Cooking Terms	10
Ingredients	12
Tools	14
Baked Fish Cakes	16
Spicy Fish Tacos	18
Crispy Fish & Chips	20
Ginger Fish Soup	22
Nutty Fish Bake	24
Fast & Easy Foil Fish	26
Curry Fish Sandwich	28
Conclusion	30
Glossary	31
Websites	31
Index	32

Get the Dish on Fish!

The main dish is where you start when planning a meal. It's the most important part. Then you choose salads, side dishes, and **desserts** to go with the main dish. Fish is a great base for many main dishes. It is a favorite meat of people all over the world. It's easy to make, tasty to eat, and there are tons of ways to prepare it!

There are many kinds of fish and many ways to cook it. Fry up some fish 'n' chips. Bake a tasty fish and veggies meal. Chow down on some Mexican fish tacos.

Try all of the fish recipes in this book. Then think of your own ways to cook fish. The possibilities are endless!

I ♥ FISH

what's not to love about fish?

It makes a great meal with the right preparation. Here are a few tips and tricks to make your fish dishes even better.

PICKING THE MEAT

Most supermarkets have a fresh fish section. A fresh fish should not have a strong odor. It should smell fresh, like the ocean. If it smells really fishy or like **ammonia**, do not buy it.

FREEZING UP

Use fresh seafood right away or freeze it. Before you use it, **thaw** it overnight in the refrigerator.

HANDLING THE MEAT
Wash **thawed** fish under running water. Pat it dry with a **towel**.

KEEP IT CLEAN
Wash your hands before and after touching the fish. Wash any **utensils** that touched raw fish separately from other dishes.

BONES OUT
Some fish still have bones! Get them out before cooking the fish. Turn a bowl upside down. Lay the fish on top. The bones should poke out. Pick them out with a **tweezers**.

COOKING THE MEAT
When you bake fish, the meat turns white when it is done. If a fish is overcooked it will be tough or rubbery.

COOKING BASICS

Ask Permission

- Before you cook, ask **permission** to use the kitchen, cooking tools, and ingredients.

- If you'd like to do something yourself, say so! Just remember to be safe.

- If you would like help, ask for it!

Be Prepared

- Be organized. Knowing where everything is makes cooking safer and more fun!

- Read the directions all the way through before starting a recipe. Follow the directions in order.

- The most important ingredient is preparation! Make sure you have everything you'll need.

Be Smart, Be Safe

- Never cook if you are home alone.

- Always have an adult nearby for hot jobs, such as using the oven or the stove.

- Have an adult around when using a sharp tool, such as a knife or a grater. Always be careful when using these tools!

- Remember to turn pot handles toward the back of the stove. That way you won't accidentally knock the pots over.

Be Neat, Be Clean

- Start with clean hands, clean tools, and a clean work surface.

- Tie back long hair to keep it out of the food.

- Wear comfortable clothing and roll up your sleeves.

- Put extra ingredients and tools away when you're done.

- Wash all the dishes and **utensils**. Clean up your workspace.

COOKING TERMS

BEAT
Beat means to mix well using a whisk or electric mixer.

COAT
Coat means to cover something with another ingredient or mixture.

FLAKE
Flake means to break off small pieces of something with a fork.

SHRED
Shred means to cut small pieces of something using a grater.

SLICE
Slice means to cut something into pieces of the same thickness.

BOIL
Boil means to heat liquid until it begins to bubble.

CHOP
Chop means to cut something into small pieces.

GREASE
Grease means to coat something with butter or cooking spray.

MINCE
Mince means to cut or chop something into very tiny pieces.

STIR
Stir means to mix ingredients together, usually with a large spoon.

WHISK
Whisk means to beat quickly by hand with a whisk or a fork.

INGREDIENTS

Here are some of the ingredients you will need.

| almonds | broccoli |

| cumin | garlic | ginger root | green onions |

| paprika | Parmesan cheese | parsley | potato |

| rosemary | salmon fillets | sesame oil | soy sauce |

carrots	cayenne pepper	cheddar cheese	cod fillets

lemon juice	lettuce	mahimahi fillets	onion

red bell pepper	red curry paste	red pepper flakes	rice noodles

spinach	tomatoes	tortillas	vegetable broth

TOOLS

Here are some of the tools you will need.

aluminum foil

baking sheet

large pot

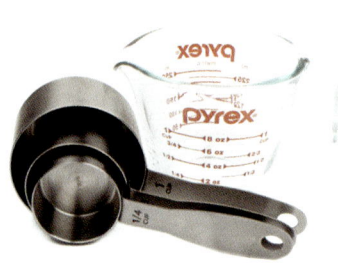
measuring cups

measuring spoons

saucepan

sharp knife

spatula

| basting brush | cutting board | fork |

| mixing bowls | mixing spoon | plate |

 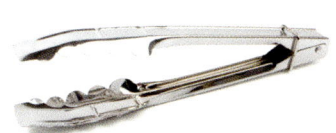 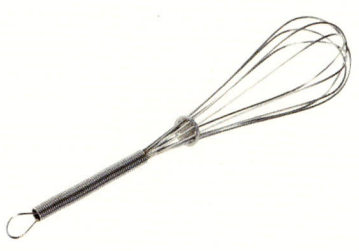

| square baking dish | tongs | whisk |

BAKED Fish Cakes

Bake some cakes, and eat them too!

Serves 5

INGREDIENTS

- 3 tablespoons olive oil
- ½-pound salmon fillet
- ¾ cup minced green onions
- ½ cup minced red bell pepper
- ¼ cup minced parsley
- 1½ teaspoons Italian seasoning
- 1 cup bread crumbs
- 1 teaspoon lemon juice
- 3 tablespoons mayonnaise
- 3 tablespoons plain yogurt
- 1 teaspoon mustard
- 2 eggs, beaten

TOOLS

- measuring spoons
- sharp knife
- cutting board
- measuring cups
- large pot
- spatula
- plate
- mixing bowl
- fork
- mixing spoon
- baking sheet
- aluminum foil
- pot holders

1. Put 2 tablespoons of oil in a large pot. Heat it over medium heat for 1 minute. Add the salmon. Cook for 5 minutes. Turn the fish over. Cook for 5 minutes. Put the fish on a plate. Let it cool.

2. Put 1 tablespoon of oil in the pot. Add the green onions, bell pepper, parsley, and seasoning. Stir and cook for 15 minutes.

3. Put the bread crumbs and vegetables in a large bowl. Flake the salmon on top. Add the remaining ingredients. Stir well. Put it in the refrigerator for 30 minutes.

4. Preheat the oven to 400 degrees. Cover the baking sheet with aluminum foil. Shape the fish mixture into four **patties**. Put them on the baking sheet. Bake for 10 minutes. Turn them over. Bake for 10 more minutes.

SPICY Fish Tacos

Make a Mexican dish with flair!

Serves 5

INGREDIENTS

- 2 tablespoons olive oil
- 2 teaspoons cumin
- 2 teaspoons paprika
- 1 teaspoon cayenne pepper
- 16-ounce cod fillet
- 10 small tortillas
- 2 cups chopped tomatoes
- 2 cups shredded cabbage
- 1½ cups shredded cheddar cheese
- ¼ cup chopped green onions
- ⅓ cup chopped avocado
- ⅓ cup sour cream

TOOLS

- measuring spoons
- sharp knife
- cutting board
- measuring cups
- saucepan
- spatula
- mixing bowls
- fork
- spoon
- pot holders

1. Put the olive oil in a small bowl. Add the cumin, paprika, and cayenne pepper. Stir the ingredients together. Put the fish in the bowl. Coat the fish with the olive oil mixture. Let it sit for 30 minutes.

2. Heat a saucepan over medium-high heat. Put the fish in the pan. Cook for 5 minutes. Turn the fish over. Cook for 4 minutes.

3. Put the fish in a clean bowl. Use a fork to break it into small pieces.

4. Heat each tortilla in the microwave for 20 seconds. Put a spoonful each of fish, tomatoes, cabbage, and cheese on each tortilla.

5. Top each taco with green onions, avocado, and sour cream.

CRISPY Fish & Chips

Make a tasty classic meal!

INGREDIENTS

- 2 potatoes
- 2 tablespoons vegetable oil
- 1 egg
- 1 tablespoon lemon juice
- ¾ cup bread crumbs
- ¼ cup shredded Parmesan cheese
- 1 pound cod fillets, cut into strips

TOOLS

- measuring spoons
- measuring cups
- sharp knife
- cutting board
- baking sheets
- aluminum foil
- mixing bowls
- whisk
- plate
- pot holders

Serves 4

1. Preheat the oven to 325 degrees. Cover the baking sheets with aluminum foil.

2. Cut the potatoes into ¼-inch (1 cm) slices. Put them in a bowl. Add the vegetable oil. Coat the potatoes with the oil. Put the potatoes on a baking sheet.

3. Whisk the egg and lemon juice together in a bowl.

4. Put the bread crumbs and cheese on a plate. Coat the fish strips with the egg mixture. Then roll them in the bread crumb mixture. Pat the strips gently so the bread crumbs stick. Put the fish on the other baking sheet.

5. Put both baking sheets in the oven. Take the fish out after 30 minutes. Leave the potatoes in the oven for 10 more minutes.

GINGER Fish Soup

Slurp up an amazing soup!

Serves 4

INGREDIENTS

- 1 pound cod fillets
- 1 teaspoon black pepper
- 2 teaspoons sesame oil
- 3 cups vegetable broth
- 1 teaspoon minced ginger
- ½ teaspoon red pepper flakes
- 3 tablespoons soy sauce
- ½ teaspoon sugar
- 4 ounces rice noodles
- ⅓ cup spinach

TOOLS

- measuring spoons
- measuring cups
- sharp knife
- cutting board
- mixing bowl
- basting brush
- large pot
- mixing spoon
- pot holders

1. Cut the cod into bite-size pieces. Put the black pepper and oil in a bowl. Stir them together. Add the fish. Gently brush the pepper mixture on the fish. Let it sit for 15 minutes.

2. Put the broth, ginger, pepper flakes, soy sauce, and sugar in a large pot. Bring to a boil over high heat. Add the noodles. Cook for 2 minutes.

3. Turn the heat to medium. Add the fish and the spinach. Cook for 3 minutes.

TIP
Add 1 teaspoon of chopped parsley for a tasty **garnish**.

NUTTY Fish Bake

Make a crunchy and delicious dish!

Serves 4

INGREDIENTS

⅓ cup chopped almonds
⅓ cup bread crumbs
2 teaspoons chopped rosemary
½ teaspoon brown sugar
1 teaspoon lemon juice
¼ teaspoon salt
¼ teaspoon cayenne pepper
2 teaspoons olive oil
non-stick cooking spray
4 mahimahi fillets
1 egg white

TOOLS

measuring cups
measuring spoons
sharp knife
cutting board
square baking dish
mixing spoon
mixing bowls
whisk
basting brush
pot holders

1 Preheat the oven to 350 degrees. Put the almonds, bread crumbs, rosemary, brown sugar, lemon juice, salt, and cayenne pepper in the baking dish. Stir in the olive oil. Bake for 8 minutes.

2 Put the almond mixture in a bowl. Wash the baking dish.

3 Turn the oven up to 400 degrees. Grease the baking dish with non-stick spray.

4 Put the fish in the baking dish. Beat the egg white in a small bowl. Brush the egg over the fish.

5 Cover the fish with the almond mixture. Bake for 10 minutes.

1

4

5

FAST & EASY Foil Fish

wrap up a fresh fish meal!

Serves 4

INGREDIENTS

non-stick cooking spray
1 cod fillet
1 tablespoon olive oil
½ teaspoon salt
1 teaspoon black pepper
1 tablespoon Old Bay seasoning
½ cup chopped red bell pepper
½ cup chopped carrots
½ cup chopped onion
½ cup chopped broccoli
1 tablespoon lemon juice

TOOLS

measuring spoons
measuring cups
sharp knife
cutting board
baking sheet
aluminum foil
mixing bowl
mixing spoon
basting brush
pot holders

1. Preheat the oven to 420 degrees. Cover the baking sheet with aluminum foil. Grease the foil with non-stick spray. Put the fish on the baking sheet.

2. Put the olive oil, salt, black pepper, and Old Bay in a bowl. Stir them together. Brush the mixture on the fish.

3. Put the red peppers, carrots, onions, and broccoli around the fish. Drizzle the lemon juice on top.

4. Put aluminum foil over the fish and vegetables. Roll the edges of the foil together all the way around.

5. Bake the fish and vegetables for 15 minutes.

CURRY Fish Sandwich

Make a fish sandwich with a twist!

Serves 4

INGREDIENTS

1 teaspoon red curry paste
½ teaspoon sea salt
4 tablespoons olive oil
4 small salmon fillets
1 medium onion, chopped
1 teaspoon minced garlic
1 tablespoon mustard
8 slices bread
4 leaves lettuce
1 tomato, sliced

TOOLS

measuring spoons
sharp knife
cutting board
small bowl
mixing spoon
plate
basting brush
large pot
dinner knife
tongs
dinner knife
pot holders

1. Put the red curry paste, sea salt, and 2 tablespoons of olive oil in a small bowl. Stir them together. Put the fish on a plate. Brush the mixture over the fish. Let it sit for 20 minutes.

2. Put the onions, garlic, and 2 tablespoons of olive oil in a large pot. Heat it over medium heat for 10 minutes.

3. Add the fish to the pot. Cook for 5 minutes. Turn the fish over. Cook for 3 more minutes.

4. Spread mustard on two slices of bread. Lay a lettuce leaf and tomato slice on top of one slice. Add a fish **fillet**. Lay the second bread slice on top.

5. Repeat step 4 to make three more sandwiches.

Conclusion

Explore the world of fish dishes. What else can you cook up?

Main dishes are fun to make and share! Feel proud of the dishes you prepare. Eat them with your family and friends. Fish is one of many great ingredients for main dishes. Don't stop with fish. Try other ingredients too!

Glossary

ammonia – a colorless gas or liquid that has a strong smell and is often used in cleaning products.

dessert – a sweet food, such as fruit, ice cream, or pastry, served after a meal.

fillet – a piece or slice of boneless meat or fish.

garnish – a small amount of food added to a dish, usually for decoration.

patty – a round, flat cake made with chopped or ground food.

permission – when a person in charge says it's okay to do something.

thaw – to melt or unfreeze.

towel – a cloth or paper used for cleaning or drying.

tweezers – a small tool used to grasp or pull something.

utensil – a tool used to prepare or eat food.

WEBSITES

To learn more about Cool Main Dishes, visit **booklinks.abdopublishing.com**. These links are routinely monitored and updated to provide the most current information available.

Index

A
adult help, need for, 2, 8, 9

B
baked fish, recipes for, 16, 17, 24, 25, 26, 27

C
cleanliness, guidelines for, 7, 9
creativity, in cooking, 5, 30

F
fish
   bones, 7
   choosing, 6
   cleaning, 7
   handling, 7
   storing, 6
   use in main dishes, 4, 5, 30
fish and chips, recipe for, 20, 21
fish cakes, recipe for, 16, 17
friends and family, 30

I
ingredients
   preparation of, 8, 10, 11
   types of, 12, 13

K
kitchen use, permission for, 8

M
main dishes, definition of, 4
meal planning, 4

N
nuts, allergies to, 2

P
preparation, for cooking, 8

R
recipes
   reading and following, 8
   symbols in, 2

S
safety, guidelines for, 2, 8, 9
sandwich, recipe for, 28, 29
sharp utensils, safe use of, 2, 9
soup, recipe for, 22, 23
stove and oven, safe use of, 2, 9

T
tacos, recipe for, 18, 19
terms, about cooking, 10, 11
tools and equipment, for cooking, 14, 15

W
websites, about cooking main dishes, 31

17(0)

RECEIVED JUN 20 2017